FINAL CURTAIN

FINAL CURTAIN

Ngaio Marsh

FELONY & MAYHEM PRESS • NEW YORK

All the characters and events portrayed in this work are fictitious.

FINAL CURTAIN

A Felony & Mayhem mystery

PRINTING HISTORY

First U.K. edition (Collins): 1947
First U.S. edition (Little, Brown): 1947
Felony & Mayhem edition: 2013

ISBN: 978-1-937384-57-9

Manufactured in the United States of America

Printed on 100% recycled paper

Library of Congress Cataloging-in-Publication Data

Marsh, Ngaio, 1895-1982.
Final curtain / Ngaio Marsh.
    p. cm.
"A Felony & Mayhem mystery."
ISBN 978-1-937384-57-9 (trade pbk.) -- ISBN 978-1-937384-48-7 (ebook)
1. Alleyn, Roderick (Fictitious character)--Fiction. 2. Police--England-
-Fiction. 3. Mystery fiction. I. Title.
PR9639.3.M27F56 2013
823'.912--dc23
                        2012031694

For Joan and Cecil
with my love

CAST OF CHARACTERS

Agatha Troy Alleyn

Katti Bostock

Nigel Bathgate

Sir Henry Ancred, Bart

Claude Ancred, *his elder son, absent*

Thomas Ancred, *his younger son*

Pauline Kentish, *his elder daughter*

Paul Kentish
Patricia Kentish (Panty) } *his grandchildren*

Desdemona Ancred, *his younger daughter*

Millamant Ancred, *his daughter-in-law (wife to Henry Irving, deceased)*

Cedric Ancred, *his heir apparent*

The Hon Mrs Claude Ancred (Jenetta), *his daughter-in-law*
   (wife to Claude Ancred)

Fenella Ancred, *her daughter*

Miss Sonia Orrincourt

Miss Caroline Able

Barker, *Butler at Ancreton Manor*

Dr Withers, *GP at Ancreton*

Mr Juniper, *Chemist*

Mr Rattisbon, *Solicitor*

Mr Mortimer, *Of Mortimer & Loame, Undertakers and Embalmers*

Roderick Alleyn, Chief
   Detective-Inspector
Detective-Inspector Fox
Detective-Sergeant Bailey
Dr Curtis, Police Surgeon
Detective-Sergeant Thompson
Village Constable

} *Of the Criminal Investigation Department, New Scotland Yard*

The icon above says you're holding a copy of a book in the Felony & Mayhem "Vintage" category. These books were originally published prior to about 1965, and feature the kind of twisty, ingenious puzzles beloved by fans of Agatha Christie and John Dickson Carr. If you enjoy this book, you may well like other "Vintage" titles from Felony & Mayhem Press.

Other "Vintage" titles from

FELONY&MAYHEM

NGAIO MARSH (con't)
False Scent
Hand in Glove
Dead Water
Killer Dolphin
Clutch of Constables
When in Rome
Tied Up in Tinsel
Black as He's Painted
Last Ditch
A Grave Mistake
Photo Finish
Light Thickens
Collected Short Mysteries

PATRCIA MOYES
Dead Men Don't Ski
The Sunken Sailor
Death on the Agenda
Murder à la Mode
Falling Star
Johnny Under Ground
Murder Fantastical
Death and the Dutch Uncle
Who Saw Her Die?
Season of Snow and Sins

*The Curious Affair
of the Third Dog*
Black Widower
The Coconut Killings
Who Is Simon Warwick
Angel Death
A Six-Letter Word for Death

LENORE GLEN OFFORD
Skeleton Key
The Glass Mask
The Smiling Tiger
My True Love Lies
The 9 Dark Hours

SS VAN DINE
The Benson Murder Case
The Canary Murder Case
The Greene Murder Case
The Bishop Murder Case
The Scarab Murder Case
The Kennel Murder Case
The Casino Murder Case
The Dragon Murder Case

For more about these books, and other Felony & Mayhem titles, or to place an order, please visit our website at:

www.FelonyAndMayhem.com

FINAL CURTAIN

CHAPTER ONE

Siege of Troy

'CONSIDERED SEVERALLY,' said Troy, coming angrily into the studio, 'a carbuncle, a month's furlough and a husband returning from the antipodes don't sound like the ingredients of a hell-brew. Collectively, they amount to precisely that.'

Katti Bostock stepped heavily back from her easel, screwed up her eyes, and squinting dispassionately at her work said: 'Why?'

'They've telephoned from CI. Rory's on his way. He'll probably get here in about three weeks. By which time I shall have returned, cured of my carbuncle, to the girls in the back room.'

'At least,' said Miss Bostock, scowling hideously at her work, 'he won't have to face the carbuncle. There is that.'

'It's on my hip.'

'I know that, you owl.'

'Well—but, Katti,' Troy argued, standing beside her friend, 'you will allow and must admit, it's a stinker. You *are* going it,' she added, squinting at Miss Bostock's canvas.

'You'll have to move into the London flat a bit earlier, that's all.'

'But if only the carbuncle, and Rory and my leave had come together—well, the carbuncle a bit earlier, certainly— we'd have had a fortnight down here together. The AC promised us that. Rory's letters have been full of it. It is tough, Katti, you can't deny it. And if you so much as look like saying there are worse things in Europe—'

'All right, all right,' said Miss Bostock, pacifically. 'I was only going to point out that it's reasonably lucky your particular back room and Roderick's job both happen to be in London. Look for the silver lining, dear,' she added unkindly. 'What's that letter you keep taking in and out of your pocket?'

Troy opened her thin hand and disclosed a crushed sheet of notepaper. 'That?' she murmured. 'Oh, yes, there's that. You never heard anything so dotty. Read it.'

'It's got cadmium red all over it.'

'I know. I dropped it on my palette. It's on the back, luckily.'

Miss Bostock spread out the letter on her painting-table, adding several cobalt finger-prints in the process. It was a single sheet of pre-war notepaper, thick, white, with an engraved heading surmounted by a crest—a cross with fluted extremities.

'Crikey!' said Miss Bostock. 'Ancreton Manor. That's the—Crikey!' Being one of those people who invariably read letters aloud she began to mutter:

Miss Agatha Troy (Mrs Roderick Alleyn)
Tatlers End House
Bossicote, Bucks.

Dear Madam,
My father-in-law, Sir Henry Ancred, asks me to write to you in reference to a portrait of himself in the character of Macbeth, for which he would be pleased

to engage your services. The picture is to hang in the entrance hall at Ancreton Manor, and will occupy a space six by four feet in dimension. As he is in poor health he wishes the painting to be done here, and will be pleased if you can arrange to stay with us from Saturday, November 17th, until such time as the portrait is completed. He presumes this will be in about a week. He will be glad to know, by telegram, whether this arrangement will suit you, and also your fee for such a commission.

I am,

Yours faithfully,

MILLAMANT ANCRED.

'Well,' said Miss Bostock, 'of all the cheek!'

Troy grinned. 'You'll notice I'm to dodge up a canvas six by four in seven days. I wonder if he expects me to throw in the three witches and the Bloody Child.'

'Have you answered it?'

'Not yet,' Troy mumbled.

'It was written six days ago,' scolded Miss Bostock.

'I know. I must. How shall I word the telegram: "Deeply regret am not house painter"?'

Katti Bostock paused, her square fingers still planted under the crest. 'I thought only peers had those things peppered about on their notepaper,' she said.

'You'll notice it's a cross, with ends like an anchor. Hence Ancred, one supposes.'

'Oh! I say!' said Katti, rubbing her nose with her blue finger. 'That's funny.'

'What is?'

'Didn't you do a set of designs for that production of *Macbeth*?'

'I did. That may have given them the idea.'

'Good Lord! Do you remember,' said Miss Bostock, 'we saw him in the play. You and Roderick, and I? The Bathgates took us. Before the war.'

'Of course I do,' said Troy. 'He was magnificent, wasn't he?'

'What's more, he looked magnificent. *What* a head. Troy, do you remember, we said—'

'So we did. Katti,' said Troy, 'you're *not* by any chance going to suggest—'

'No, no, of course not. Good Lord, no! But it's rum that we did say it would be fun to have a go at him in the grand manner. Against the backcloth they did from your design; lolloping clouds and a black simplified castle form. The figure cloaked and dim.'

'He wouldn't thank you for that, I dare say. The old gentleman probably wishes to appear in a flash of lightning, making faces. Well, I'd better send the telegram. Oh, damn!' Troy sighed. 'I wish I could settle down to something.'

Miss Bostock glowered thoughtfully at Troy. Four years of intensive work at pictorial surveys for the army, followed by similar and even more exacting work for UNRRA, had, she thought, tried her friend rather high. She was thin and a bit jumpy. She'd be better if she could do more painting, thought Katti, who did not regard the making of pictorial maps, however exquisite, as full compensation for the loss of pure art. Four years' work with little painting and no husband. 'Thank God,' Katti thought, 'I'm different, I get along nicely.'

'If he gets here in three weeks,' Troy was saying, 'where do you suppose he is now? He might be in New York. But he'd cable if he was in New York. The last letter was still from New Zealand, of course. And the cable.'

'Why don't you get on with your work?'

'Work?' said Troy vaguely. 'Oh, well. I'll send off that telegram.' She wandered to the door and came back for the letter. 'Six by four,' she said. 'Imagine it!'

❋ ❋ ❋

'Mr Thomas Ancred?' said Troy, looking at the card in her hand. 'My dear Katti, he's actually *here* on the spot.'

Katti, who had almost completed her vigorous canvas, laid down her brushes and said: 'This is in answer to your telegram. He's come to badger you. Who is he?'

'A son of Sir Henry Ancred's, I fancy. Isn't he a theatrical producer? I seem to remember seeing: "Produced by Thomas Ancred" under casts of characters. Yes, of course he is. That production of *Macbeth* we were talking about at the Unicorn. He was in the picture somewhere then. Look, there's Unicorn Theatre scribbled on the card. We'll have to ask him to dinner, Katti. There's not a train before nine. That'll mean opening another tin. *What* a bore.'

'I don't see why he need stay. There's a pub in the village. If he chooses to come on a fool's errand!'

'I'll see what he's like.'

'Aren't you going to take off that painting smock?'

'I don't suppose so,' Troy said vaguely, and walked up the path from her studio to her house. It was a cold afternoon. Naked trees rattled in a north wind and leaden clouds hurried across the sky. 'Suppose,' Troy pretended, 'I was to walk in and find it was Rory. Suppose he'd kept it a secret and there he was waiting in the library. He'd have lit the fire so that it should be there for us to meet by. His face would be looking like it did the first time he stood there, a bit white with excitement. Suppose—' She had a lively imagination and she built up her fantasy quickly, warming her thoughts at it. So clear was her picture that it brought a physical reaction; her heart knocked, her hand, even, trembled a little as she opened the library door.

The man who stood before the unkindled hearth was tall and stooped a little. His hair, which had the appearance of floss, stood up thinly like a child's. He wore glasses and blinked behind them at Troy.

'Good afternoon,' he said. 'I'm Thomas Ancred, but of course you know that because of the card. I hope you don't mind my coming. I didn't really want to, but the family insisted.'

He held out his hand, but didn't do anything with it when Troy took it, so that she was obliged to give it a slight squeeze and let it go. 'The whole thing's silly,' he said. 'About Papa's portrait, I mean, of course. We call him "Papa," you know. Some people think it sounds affected; but there it is. About Papa's portrait. I must tell you they all got a great shock when your telegram came. They rang me up. They said you couldn't have understood, and I was to come and explain.'

Troy lit the fire. 'Do sit down,' she said, 'you must be frozen. What did they think I hadn't understood?'

'Well, first of all, that it was an honour to paint Papa. I told them that it would have been the other way round, if anything, supposing you'd consented. Thank you, I will sit down. It's quite a long walk from the station and I think I've blistered my heel. Do you mind if I have a look? I can feel through my sock, you know.'

'Look away,' said Troy.

'Yes,' said Thomas after a pause, 'it is a blister. I'll just keep my toe in my shoe for manners and I dare say the blister will go down. About my father. Of course you know he's the Grand Old Man of the British stage so I needn't go into all that. Do you admire his acting at all?'

'A great deal,' said Troy. She was glad that the statement was truthful. This curious man, she felt, would have recognized a polite evasion.

'*Do you?*' he said. 'That's nice. He is quite good, of course, though a little creaky at times, don't you feel? And then, all those mannerisms! He can't play an emotional bit, you know, without sucking in his breath rather loudly. But he really is good in a magnificent Mrs Beeton sort of way. A recipe for everything and only the best ingredients used.'

'Mr Ancred,' Troy said, 'what is all this about?'

'Well, it's part of the build-up. It's supposed to make you see things in a different light. The great British actor painted by the great British artist, don't you know? And although I don't suppose you'd *like* Ancreton much it might amuse you to see it. It's very baronial. The portrait would hang under the minstrels' gallery with special lighting. He doesn't mind what he pays. It's to commemorate his seventy-fifth birthday. His own idea is that the nation ought to have given it to him, but as the nation doesn't seem to have thought of that he's giving it to himself. And to posterity of course,' Thomas added as an after-thought, cautiously slipping his finger inside his loosened shoe.

'If you'd like me to suggest one or two painters who might—'

'Some people prick blisters,' said Thomas, 'but I don't. No, thank you, they've made a second-best list. I was telling you about Ancreton. You know those steel engravings of castles and halls in Victorian books? All turrets and an owl flying across the moon? That's Ancreton. It was built by my great-grandfather. He pulled down a nice Queen Anne house and erected Ancreton. There was a moat but people got diph-theria so it was let go and they're growing vegetables in it. The food is quite good, because there are lots of vegetables, and Papa cut down the Great East Spinney during the war and stored the wood, so there are still fires.'

Thomas smiled at his hostess. He had a tentative sidelong smile. 'Yes,' he said, 'that's Ancreton. I expect you'd hate it, but you couldn't help laughing.'

'As I'm not going, however—' Troy began with a rising sense of panic.

But Thomas continued unmoved. 'And then, of course, there's the family. Well! Papa and Millamant and Pauline and Panty to begin with. Are you at all keen on the emotions?'

'I haven't an idea what you mean.'

'My family is very emotional. They feel everything most deeply. The funny thing about *that*,' said Thomas, 'is that they really do feel deeply. They really are sensitive, only people are inclined to think nobody could really be as sensitive as they seem to be, so that's hard luck on the family.' Thomas took off his spectacles and gazed at Troy with short-sighted inno-cence. 'Except,' he added, 'that they have the satisfaction of knowing that they are so much more sensitive than any one else. That's a point that might interest you.'

'Mr Ancred,' Troy said patiently, 'I am on leave because I've not been well—'

'Indeed? You look all right. What's the matter with you?'

'A carbuncle,' said Troy angrily.

'Really?' said Thomas clucking his tongue. 'How sickening for you.'

'—and in consequence I'm not at the top of my form. A commission of the sort mentioned in your sister-in-law's letter would take at least three weeks' intensive work. The letter gives me a week.'

'How long is your leave?'

Troy bit her lips. 'That's not the point,' she said. 'The point is—'

'I had a carbuncle once. You feel better if you keep on with your job. Less depressed. Mine,' said Thomas proudly, 'was on my bottom. Now that *is* awkward.' He looked inquiringly at Troy, who by this time, according to her custom, was sitting on the hearth-rug. 'Obviously,' Thomas continued, 'yours—'

'It's on my hip. It's very much better—'

'Well, then —'

'—but that's not the point. Mr Ancred, I can't accept this commission. My husband is coming home after three years' absence—'

'When?' Thomas asked instantly.

'As far as we know in three weeks,' said Troy, wishing she could bring herself to lie freely to her visitor. 'But one can never tell. It might be sooner.'

'Well, of course Scotland Yard will let you know about that, won't they. Because, I mean, he's pretty high up, isn't he? Supposing you did go to Ancreton, they could ring you up there just as well as here.'

'The point is,' Troy almost shouted, 'I don't want to paint your father as Macbeth. I'm sorry to put it so bluntly, but I just don't.'

'I told them you wouldn't,' said Thomas complacently. 'The Bathgates thought they knew better.'

'The Bathgates? Do you mean Nigel and Angela Bathgate?'

'Who else? Nigel and I are old friends. When the family started all this business I went to see him and asked if he thought you'd do it. Nigel said he knew you were on leave, and he thought it would be nice for you.'

'He knows nothing whatever about it.'

'He said you liked meeting queer people. He said you'd revel in Papa as a subject and gloat over his conversation. It only shows you how little we understand our friends, doesn't it?'

'Yes,' said Troy, 'it does.'

'But I can't help wondering what you'd make of Panty.'

Troy had by this time determined to ask Thomas Ancred no questions whatever, and it was with a sense of impotent fury that she heard her own voice: 'Did you say "Panty"?'

'She's my niece, you know. My sister Pauline's youngest. We call her Panty because her bloomers are always coming down. She's a Difficult Child. Her school, which is a school for Difficult Children, was evacuated to Ancreton. They are quartered in the west wing under a *very* nice person called Caroline Able. Panty is frightful.'

'Oh,' said Troy, as he seemed to expect some comment.

'Yes, indeed. She's so awful that I rather like her. She's a little girl with two pigtails and a devilish face. This sort of thing.'

Thomas put his long forefingers at right angles to his head, scowled abominably and blew out his cheeks. His eyes glittered. Much against her will, Troy was suddenly confronted with the face of a bad child. She laughed shortly. Thomas rubbed his hands. 'If I were to tell you,' he said, 'of the things that little girl does, you would open your eyes. Well, a cactus, for instance, in Sonia's bed! Unfortunately she's Papa's favourite, which makes control almost impossible. And, of course, one mustn't beat her except in anger, because that's not proper child psychology.'

He stared thoughtfully into the fire. 'Then there's Pauline, my eldest sister; she's the important type. And Milly, my sister-in-law, who perpetually laughs at nothing and housekeeps for Papa, since her husband, my eldest brother, Henry Irving, died.'

'Henry Irving!' Troy ejaculated, thinking with alarm: 'Evidently he's mad.'

'Henry Irving Ancred, of course. Papa had a great admiration for Irving, and regards himself as his spiritual successor, so he called Hal after him. And then there's Sonia. Sonia is Papa's mistress.' Thomas cleared his throat old-maid-ishly. 'Rather a Biblical situation really. You remember David and Abishag the Shunammite? They all dislike Sonia. I must say she's a *very* bad actress. Am I boring you?'

Troy, though not bored, was extremely reluctant to say so. She muttered: 'Not at all,' and offered Thomas a drink. He replied: 'Yes, thank you, if you've got plenty.' She went off to fetch it, hoping in the interim to sort out her reactions to her visitor. She found Katti Bostock in the dining-room.

'For pity's sake, Katti,' said Troy, 'come back with me. I've got a sort of monster in there.'

'Is it staying to dinner?'

'I haven't asked it, but I should think so. So we shall have to open one of Rory's tins.'

'Hadn't you better go back to this bloke?'

'Do come too. I'm afraid of him. He tells me about his family, presenting each member of it in a repellent light, and yet expecting me to desire nothing more than their acquaintance. And the alarming thing is, Katti, that the narrative has its horrid fascination. Important Pauline, acquisitive Sonia; dreadful little Panty, and Milly, who laughs perpetually at nothing; that's Millamant, of course, who wrote the letter. And Papa, larger than life, and presenting himself with his own portrait because the Nation hasn't come up to scratch—'

'You aren't going to tell me you've accepted!'

'Not I. Good Lord, no! I'd be demented. But—keep an eye on me, Katti,' said Troy.

❋ ❋ ❋

Thomas accepted the invitation to dinner, expressing himself as delighted with his share of tinned New Zealand crayfish. 'We've got friends in New Zealand and America too,' he said, 'but unfortunately tinned fish brings on an attack of Papa's gastroenteritis. If we have it he can't resist it, and so Milly doesn't let us have it. Next time I go to Ancreton she's giving me several tins to take back to my flat.'

'You don't live at Ancreton?' Troy asked.

'How could I when my job's in London? I go there sometimes for weekends to give them all an opportunity of confiding in me. Papa likes us to go. He's having quite a party for his birthday. Pauline's son, Paul, who has a wounded leg, will be there, and Millamant's son, Cedric, who is a dress-designer. I don't think you'd care for Cedric. And my sister Desdemona, who is at liberty just now, though she hopes to be cast for a part in a new play at the Crescent. My other sister-in-law, Jenetta, will be there too, I hope, with her daughter, Fenella. Her husband, my eldest brother Claude, is a Colonel in the occupation forces and hasn't come home yet.'

'Rather a large party,' said Katti. 'Fun for you.'

'There'll be a good many rows, of course,' Thomas replied. 'When you get two or three Ancreds gathered together they are certain to hurt each other's feelings. That's where I come in handy, because I'm the insensitive one and they talk to me about each other. And about Sonia, I needn't say. We shall all talk about Sonia. We'd hoped to unveil your portrait of Papa on this occasion,' he said, looking wistfully at Troy. 'Indeed, that's really what the party's for.'

Troy mumbled something indistinguishable.

'Papa had a lovely time last week looking out the Macbeth clothes,' Thomas continued. 'I wonder if you remember his costume. Motley did it for us. It's red, a Paul Veroniseish red, dark but clear, with a smoky overcloak. We've got a miniature theatre at Ancreton, you know. I brought down the original backdrop for one of the inset scenes and hung it. It's quite a coincidence, isn't it,' Thomas went on innocently, 'that you did the original designs for that production? Of course, you remember the one I mean. It's very simple. A boldly distorted castle form seen in silhouette. He dressed himself and stood in front of it, resting on his claymore with his head stooped, as if listening. "Good things of day begin to droop and drowse," do you remember?'

Troy remembered that line very well. It was strange that he should have recalled it; for Alleyn was fond of telling her how, in the small hours of a stormy morning, a constable on night duty had once quoted it to him. Thomas, speaking the line, with an actor's sense of its value, sounded like an echo of her husband, and her thoughts were filled with memories of his voice.

'— He's been ill off and on for some time,' Thomas was saying, 'and gets very depressed. But the idea of the portrait bucked him up no end, and he's set his heart on you to paint it. You see, you did his hated rival.'

'Sir Benjamin Corporal?' Troy muttered, eyeing Katti.

'Yes. And old Ben makes a great story about how you only paint subjects that you take a fancy to—pictorially, I mean. He told us you took a great fancy to him pictorially. He said he was the only actor you'd ever wanted to paint.'

'On the contrary,' Troy said angrily. 'It was a commission from his native town—Huddersfield. Old popinjay!'

'He told Papa he'd only be snubbed if he approached you. Actually, Papa was dressed as Macbeth when your telegram arrived. He said: "Ah! This is propitious. Do you think, my dear, that Miss Troy—should he have said 'Mrs Alleyn?'— will care for this pose?" He was quite young-looking when he said it. And then he opened your telegram. He took it rather well, really. He just gave it to Milly, and said: "I shouldn't have put on these garments. It was always an unlucky piece. I'm a vain old fool." And he went away and changed and had an attack of gastroenteritis, poor thing. It must almost be time I thought of walking back to the station, mustn't it?'

'I'll drive you,' Troy said.

Thomas protested mildly, but Troy overruled him brusquely when the time came, and went off to start her car. Thomas said goodbye politely to Katti Bostock.

'You're a clever chap, Mr Ancred,' said Katti grimly.

'Oh, do you think so?' asked Thomas, blinking modestly. 'Oh, no! Clever? Me? Goodness, no. Goodnight. It's been nice to meet you.'

Katti waited for half an hour before she heard the sound of the returning car. Presently the door opened and Troy came in. She wore a white overcoat. A lock of her short dark hair hung over her forehead. Her hands were jammed in her pockets. She walked self-consciously down the room looking at Katti out of the corners of her eyes.

'Got rid of your rum friend?' asked Miss Bostock.

Troy cleared her throat. 'Yes. He's talked himself off.'

'Well,' said Miss Bostock, after a long silence, 'when do you leave for Ancreton?'

'Tomorrow,' said Troy shortly.

CHAPTER TWO

Departure

TROY WISHED THAT Thomas Ancred would say
goodbye and leave her to savour the moment of departure.
She enjoyed train journeys enormously, and, in these days, not
a second of the precious discomfort should be left unrelished.
But there stood Thomas on the Euston platform with nothing
to say, and filled, no doubt, with the sense of tediousness that
is inseparable from these occasions. 'Why doesn't he take off
his hat and walk away,' Troy thought fretfully. But when she
caught his eye, he gave her such an anxious smile that she
instantly felt obliged to reassure him.

'I have been wondering,' Thomas said, 'if, after all, you
will merely loathe my family.'

'In any case I shall be working.'

'Yes,' he agreed, looking immensely relieved, 'there *is*
that. I can't tell you how much I dislike many actors, and
yet, when I begin to work with them, sometimes I quite love
them. If they do what I tell them, of course.'

'Are you working this morning?' And she thought: how unreal the activities seem of people one leaves behind on railway stations.

'Yes,' said Thomas, 'a first rehearsal.'

'Please don't wait,' she said for the fourth time, and for the fourth time he replied: 'I'll just see you off,' and looked at his watch. Doors were slammed farther down the train. Troy leant out of the window. At last she was off. A man in uniform, peering frenziedly into carriage after carriage, was working his way towards her. 'Nigel!' Troy shouted. 'Nigel!'

'Oh, God, there you are!' cried Nigel Bathgate. 'Hallo, Thomas! Here! Troy! I knew I wouldn't have time to talk so I've written.' He thrust a fat envelope at her. A whistle blew. The train clunked, and Thomas said: 'Well, goodbye; they *will* be pleased;' raised his hat and slid out of view. Nigel walked rapidly along beside the window. 'What a go! You will laugh,' he said. 'Is this a novel?' Troy asked, holding up the envelope. 'Almost! You'll see.' Nigel broke into a run. 'I've always wanted to—you'll see—when's Roderick—?' 'Soon!' Troy cried. 'In three weeks!' 'Goodbye! I can't run any more.' He had gone.

Troy settled down. A young man appeared in the corridor. He peered in at the door and finally entered the already crowded carriage. With a slight twittering noise he settled himself on his upturned suitcase, with his back to the door, and opened an illustrated paper. Troy noticed that he wore a jade ring on his first finger, a particularly bright green hat and suede shoes. The other passengers looked dull and were also preoccupied with their papers. Rows of backyards and occasional heaps of rubble would continue for some time in the world outside the window pane. She sighed luxuriously, thought how much easier it would be to wait for her husband now that she was forced to paint, fell into a brief day-dream, and finally opened Nigel's letter.

Three sheets of closely typed reporter's paper fell out, together with a note written in green ink.

'13 hours, GMT,' Nigel had written. 'Troy, my dear, two hours ago Thomas Ancred, back from his visit to you, rang me up in a triumph. You're in for a party but the GOM will be grand to paint. I've always died to write up the Ancreds but can't afford the inevitable libel action. So I've amused myself by dodging up the enclosed *jeu d'esprit*. It may serve to fill in your journey. NB.'

The typescript was headed: 'Note on Sir Henry Ancred, Bart and his Immediate Circle.' 'Do I want to read it?' Troy wondered. 'It was charming of Nigel to write it, but I'm in for two weeks of the Ancreds and Thomas's commentary was exhaustive.' And she let the pages fall in her lap. At the same time the young man on the suitcase lowered his modish periodical, and stared fixedly at her. He impressed her disagreeably. His eyes suggested a kind of dull impertinence. Under the line of hair on his lip his mouth was too fresh, and projected too far above a small white chin. Everything about him was over-elegant, Troy thought, and dismissed him as an all-too-clearly-defined type. He continued to stare at her. 'If he was opposite,' she thought, 'he would begin to ask questions about the windows. What does he want?' She lifted the sheets of Nigel's typescript and began to read.

❀ ❀ ❀

'Collectively and severally,' Nigel had written, 'the Ancreds, all but one, are over-emotionalized. Any one attempting to describe or explain their behaviour must keep this characteristic firmly in mind, for without it they would scarcely exist. Sir Henry Ancred is perhaps the worst of the lot, but, because he is an actor, his friends accept his behaviour as part of his stock-in-trade, and apart from an occasional feeling of shyness in his presence, seldom make the mistake of worrying about him. Whether he was drawn to his wife (now deceased) by the discovery of a similar trait in her character, or whether, by the phenomenon of marital acclimatization, Lady Ancred learnt to exhibit emotion with a virtuosity equal to that of her husband, cannot be discovered. It can only be recorded that she did so; and died.

'Their elder daughters, Pauline (Ancred played in *The Lady of Lyons* in '96) and Desdemona (*Othello*, 1909), and their sons, Henry Irving (Ancred played a bit-part in *The Bells*) and Claude (Pauline's twin) in their several modes, have inherited or acquired the emotional habit. Only Thomas (Ancred was resting in 1904 when Thomas was born) is free of it. Thomas, indeed, is uncommonly placid. Perhaps for this reason his parent, sisters, and brothers appeal to him when they hurt each other's feelings, which they do punctually, two or three times a week, and always with an air of tragic astonishment.

'Pauline, Claude, and Desdemona, in turn, followed their father's profession. Pauline joined a northern repertory company, married John Kentish, a local man of property, retired upon provincial glories more enduring than those she was likely to enjoy as an actress, and gave birth to Paul and, twelve years later, Patricia (born 1936 and known as Panty). Like all Ancred's children, except Thomas, Pauline was extremely handsome, and has retained her looks.

'Claude, her twin, drifted from Oriel into the OUDS, and thence, on his father's back, into romantic juveniles. He married the Hon Miss Jenetta Cairnes, who had a fortune, but never, he is fond of saying, has understood him. She is an intelligent woman. They have one daughter, Fenella.

'Desdemona, Sir Henry's fourth child (aged thirty-six at the time of this narrative), has become a good emotional actress, difficult to place, as she has a knack of cracking the seams of the brittle slickly drawn roles for which West-End managements, addled by her beauty, occasionally cast her. She has become attached to a Group, and appears in pieces written by two surrealists, uttering her lines in such a heart-rending manner that they seem, even to Desdemona herself, to be fraught with significance. She is unmarried and has suffered a great deal from two unhappy love affairs.

'The eldest son, Henry Irving Ancred, became a small-part actor and married Mildred Cooper, whom his father promptly re-christened Millamant, as at that time he was engaged upon a revival of *The Way of the World*. Millamant she has remained, and, before her husband died, gave birth to a son, Cedric, about whom the less said the better.

'Your friend, Thomas, is unmarried. Having discovered, after two or three colourless ventures, that he was a bad actor, he set about teaching himself to become a good producer. In this, after a struggle, he succeeded, and is now established as director for Incorporated Playhouses, Limited, Unicorn Theatre. He has never been known to lose his temper at rehearsals, but may sometimes be observed, alone in the stalls, rocking to and fro with his head in his hands. He lives in a bachelor's flat in Westminster.

'All these offspring, Pauline, Claude, Desdemona and Thomas, their sister-in-law, Millamant, and their children, are like details in a design, the central motive of which is Sir Henry himself. Sir Henry, known to his associates as the GOM of the Stage, is believed to be deeply attached to his family. That is part of his legend, and the belief may be founded in fact. He sees a great deal of his family, and perhaps it would be accurate to say that he loves best those particular members of it of whom, at any given moment, he sees least. His wife he presumably loved. They never quarrelled and always sided together against whichever of their young had wounded the feelings of one or the other of them. Thomas was the exception to this, as he is to most other generalities one might apply to the Ancreds.

'"Old Tommy!" Sir Henry will say. "Funny chap! Never quite know where you are with him. T'uh!" This scarcely articulated noise, "T'uh," is used by all the Ancreds (except, of course, Thomas) to express a kind of disillusioned resignation. It's uttered on a high note and is particularly characteristic.

'Sir Henry is not a theatrical knight but a baronet, having inherited his title, late in life, from an enormously wealthy second cousin. It's a completely obscure baronetcy, and, although perfectly genuine, difficult to believe in. Perhaps this is because he himself is so obviously impressed by it and likes to talk about Norman ancestors with names that sound as if they'd been chosen from the dramatis personae in a Lyceum programme, the Sieur D'Ancred, and so on. His crest is on everything. He looks, as his dresser is fond of saying, every inch the aristocrat—silver hair, hook nose, blue eyes. Up to a few years ago he still appeared in drawing-room comedies, giving exquisite performances of charming or irascible buffers. Sometimes he forgot his lines, but, by the use of a number of famous mannerisms, diddled his audiences into believing it was a lesser actor who had slipped. His last Shakespearian appearance was as Macbeth on the Bard's birthday, at the age of sixty-eight. He then developed a chronic gastric disorder and retired from the stage to his family seat, Ancreton, which in its architectural extravagances may possibly remind him of Dunsinane.

'There he remains, guarded by Millamant, who, since the death of her husband, has house-kept for her father-in-law, and who is supposed by the rest of her family to be feathering a nest for her son, the egregious Cedric, who is delicate. The family (excepting Thomas) is inclined to laugh with bitter emphasis when Cedric is mentioned, and to criticize poor Milly's treatment of the GOM. Milly is a jolly woman and laughs at them. She once told Thomas that if either of his sisters cared to take on her job she'd be delighted to relinquish it. She had them there, for though they all visit Ancreton a great deal, they invariably leave after a few days in a tempest of wounded feelings.

'Occasionally they close their ranks. They have done so at the moment, being at war, as a family, with Miss Sonia Orrincourt, an indifferent actress, with whom, at the age of seventy-five, their father is having a fling. This astounding old man has brought the lady to Ancreton, and there, it appears, she intends to remain. She is an erstwhile member of the chorus and was selected as a type to understudy a small part in a piece at the Unicorn. This was a shattering innovation. The Unicorn, in the theatre world, is as Boodles in clubland. No musical comedy artist, before Miss Orrincourt, had enlivened its stage-door. Sir Henry watched a rehearsal. In three weeks Miss Orrincourt, having proved a complete washout as an understudy, was given the sack by Thomas. She then sought out his father, wept on his waistcoat, and reappeared in her present unmistakable role at Ancreton. She is a blonde. Pauline and Desdemona say that she is holding out on the Old Man with a view to matrimony. Thomas believes her to have taken the more complaisant attitude. Claude, in the Middle East, has sent a cable so guarded in its phrases that the only thing it makes clear is his rage. Claude's wife, Jenetta, a shrewd and amusing woman, who maintains a detached attitude to her relations-by-marriage, has been summoned, in Claude's absence, to a conclave. It is possible that her only child, Fenella, hitherto a second favourite with Sir Henry after Pauline's child Panty, might lose ground if he married. Even jolly Millamant is shaken. Her appalling Cedric is the senior grandson, and Sir Henry has of late begun to drop disconcerting hints that there is life in the old dog yet.

'This, then, is the set-up at Ancreton. My information has come by way of occasional visits and Thomas, who, as you will have discovered, is a talkative chap and doesn't know the meaning of the word reticence.

'In some such fashion as this, dear Troy, would I begin the novel that I dare not attempt. One word more. I understand you are to paint Sir Henry in the character of Macbeth. May I assure you that with Pauline's child Panty on the premises you will find yourself also furnished with a Bloody Child.'

❀ ❀ ❀

Troy folded the typescript, and replaced it in its envelope across which Nigel had written her name in bold characters. The young man on the suitcase stared fixedly at the envelope. She turned it face downwards on her lap. His illustrated paper hung open across his knee. She saw, with annoyance, her own photograph.

So that was what he was up to. He'd recognized her. Probably, she thought, he potters about doing fancy little drawings. He looks like it. If the other people get out before we reach Ancreton Halt, he'll introduce himself and my lovely train journey will be ruined. Damn!

The country outside the window changed to a hurrying tapestry of hedgerows, curving downs and naked trees. Troy watched it contentedly. Having allowed herself to be bamboozled into taking this commission, she had entered into a state of emotional suspension. It was deeply satisfactory to know that her husband would soon return. She no longer experienced moments of something like terror lest his three years' absence should drop like a curtain between their understanding of each other. The Commissioner had promised she should know two days beforehand of Alleyn's arrival, and in the meantime the train carried her to a job among strangers who at least would not be commonplace. But I hope, Troy thought, that their family upheaval won't interfere with the old boy's sittings. That *would* be a bore.

The train drew into a junction, and the other passengers, with the exception of the young man on the suitcase, began to collect themselves. Just what she'd feared, thought Troy. She opened her lunch-basket and a book. If I eat and read at him, she thought, that may keep him off; and she remembered Guy de Maupassant's strictures upon people who eat in the train.

Now they were off again. Troy munched her sandwiches and read the opening scene of *Macbeth*. She had decided to revisit that terrible country whose only counterpart, she thought, was to be found in Emily Brontë. This fancy pleased her, and she paused to transport the wraiths of Heathcliff and Cathy to the blasted heath or to follow Fleance over the moors to Wuthering Heights. But, if I am to paint Macbeth, she thought, I must read. And as the first inflexions in the voice of a friend who is re-met after a long absence instantly prepare us for tones that we are yet to hear, so with its opening phrases, the play, which she thought she had forgotten, returned wholly to her memory.

'Do forgive me for interrupting,' said a high-pitched voice, 'but I've been madly anxious to talk to you, and this is such a *magical* opportunity.'

The young man had slid along the seat and was now opposite. His head was tilted ingratiatingly to one side and he smiled at Troy. '*Please* don't think I'm seething with sinister intentions,' he said. 'Honestly, there's *no* need to pull the communication cord.'

'I didn't for a moment suppose there was,' said Troy.

'You are Agatha Troy, aren't you?' he continued anxiously. 'I couldn't be mistaken. I mean, it's too shatteringly coincidental, isn't it? Here I am, reading my little journal, and what should I see but a perfectly blissful photograph of you. *So* exciting and so miraculously *you*. And if I'd had the weeniest doubt left, that alarming affair you're reading would have settled it.'

Troy looked from her book to the young man. 'Macbeth?' she said. 'I'm afraid I don't understand.'

'Oh, but it was too conclusive,' he said. 'But, of course, I haven't introduced myself, have I? I'm Cedric Ancred.'

'Oh,' said Troy after a pause. 'Oh, yes. I see.'

'And then to clinch it, there was your name on that envelope. I'm afraid I peered shamelessly. But it's too exciting that you're actually going to make a picture of the Old Person in all his tatts and bobs. You can't imagine what that costume is like! And the toque! Some terrifically powerful man beat it out of solid steel for him. He's my Grandpa, you know. My mother is Millamant Ancred. My father, only promise you won't tell anyone, was Henry Irving Ancred. Imagine!'

Troy could think of nothing to say in reply to this recital and took another bite out of her sandwich.

'So, you see, I had to make myself known,' he continued with an air that Troy thought of as 'winsome.' 'I'm so burnt up always about your work, and the prospect of meeting you was absolutely tonic.'

'But how did you know,' Troy asked, 'that I was going to paint Sir Henry?'

'I rang up Uncle Thomas last night and he told me. I'd been commanded to the presence, and had decided that I couldn't face it, but immediately changed my plans. You see,' said Cedric with a boyish frankness which Troy found intolerable, 'you see, I actually try to paint. I'm with Pont et Cie and I do the designs. Of course everything's too austerity and grim nowadays, but we keep toddling.'

His suit was silver grey. His shirt was pale green, his pullover was dark green, and his tie was orange. He had rather small eyes, and in the middle of his soft round chin there was a dimple.

'If I may talk about your work,' he was saying, 'there's a quality in it that appeals to me enormously. It—how can I describe it?—its design is always consistent with its subject matter. I mean, the actual *pattern* is not something arbitrarily imposed on the subject but an inevitable consequence of it. Such integrity, always. Or am I talking nonsense?'

He was not talking complete nonsense and Troy grudgingly admitted it. There were few people with whom she cared to discuss her work. Cedric Ancred watched her for a few seconds. She had the unpleasant feeling that he sensed her distaste for him. His next move was unexpected. He ran his fingers through his hair, which was damply blond and wavy 'God!' he said. 'People! The things they say! If only one could break through, as you have. God! Why is life so perpetually bloody?'

'Oh, *dear*!' Troy thought and shut her luncheon basket. Cedric was gazing at her fixedly. Evidently she was expected to reply.

'I'm not much good,' she said, 'at generalities about life.'

'No!' he muttered and nodded his head profoundly. 'Of course not. I so agree. You are perfectly right, of course.'

Troy looked furtively at her watch. A full half-hour, she thought, before we get to Ancreton Halt and then, he's coming too.

'I'm boring you,' Cedric said loudly. 'No, don't deny it. God! I'm boring you. T'uh!'

'I just don't know how to carry on this sort of conversation, that's all.'

Cedric began to nod again.

'You were reading,' he said. 'I stopped you. One should never do that. It's an offence against the Holy Ghost.'

'I never heard such nonsense,' said Troy with spirit.

Cedric laughed gloomily. 'Go on!' he said. 'Please go on. Return to your "Blasted Heath." It's an atrociously bad play, in my opinion, but go on reading it.'

But it was not easy to read, knowing that a few inches away he was glaring at her over his folded arms. She turned a page. In a minute or two he began to sigh. 'He sighs,' thought Troy, 'like the Mock Turtle, and I think he must be mad.' Presently he laughed shortly, and, in spite of herself, Troy looked up. He was still glaring at her. He had a jade cigarette case open in his hand.

'You smoke?' he asked.

She felt certain that if she refused he would make some further peculiar scene, so she took one of his cigarettes. He lit it in silence and flung himself back in his corner.

After all, Troy thought, I've got to get on with him, somehow, and she said: 'Don't you find it extraordinarily tricky hitting on exactly the right note in fashion drawings? When one thinks of what they used to be like! There's no doubt that commercial art—'

'Prostitution!' Cedric interrupted. 'Just that. If you don't mind the initial sin it's quite amusing.'

'Do you work at all for the theatre?'

'So sweet of you to take an interest,' Cedric answered rather acidly. 'Oh, yes. My Uncle Thomas occasionally uses me. Actually I'm madly keen on it. One would have thought that with the Old Person behind one there would have been an opening. Unfortunately he is not behind me, which is so sickening. I've been cut out by the Infant Monstrosity.' He brightened a little. 'It's some comfort to know I'm the eldest grandson, of course. In my more optimistic moments I tell myself he can't leave me *completely* out of his will. My worst nightmare is the one when I dream I've inherited Ancreton. I always wake screaming. Of course, with Sonia on the tapis, almost anything may happen. You've heard about Sonia?'

Troy hesitated and he went on: 'She's the Old Person's little bit of nonsense. Immensely decorative. I can't make up my mind whether she's incredibly stupid or not, but I fear not. The others are all for fighting her, tooth and claw, but I rather think of ingratiating myself in case he does marry her. What do you think?'

Troy was wondering if it was a characteristic of all male Ancreds to take utter strangers into their confidence. But they couldn't all be as bad as Cedric. After all, Nigel Bathgate had said Cedric was frightful, and even Thomas—she thought suddenly how nice Thomas seemed in retrospect when one compared him with his nephew.

'But *do* tell me,' Cedric was saying, 'how do you mean to paint him? All beetling and black? But whatever you decide it will be marvellous. You will let me creep in and see, or are you dreadfully fierce about that?'

'Rather fierce, I'm afraid,' said Troy.

'I suspected so.' Cedric looked out of the window and immediately clasped his forehead. 'It's coming,' he said. 'Every time I brace myself for the encounter and every time, if there was a train to take me, I would rush screaming back to London. In a moment we shall see it. I can't bear it. God! That one should have to face such horrors.'

'What in the world's the matter?'

'Look!' cried Cedric, covering his eyes. 'Look! Katzenjammer Castle!'

Troy looked through the window. Some two miles away, on the crest of a hill, fully displayed, stood Ancreton.

CHAPTER THREE

Ancreton

IT WAS AN ASTONISHING building. A Victorian architect, fortified and encouraged by the Ancred of his day, had pulled down a Queen Anne house and, from its rubble, caused to rise up a sublimation of his most exotic day-dreams. To no one style or period did Ancreton adhere. Its facade bulged impartially with Norman, Gothic, Baroque and Rococo excrescences. Turrets sprouted like wens from every corner. Towers rose up from a multiplicity of battlements. Arrow slits peered furtively at exopthalmic bay-windows, and out of a kaleidoscope field of tiles rose a forest of variegated chimney-stacks. The whole was presented, not against the sky, but against a dense forest of evergreen trees, for behind Ancreton crest rose another and steeper hillside, richly planted in conifers. Perhaps the imagination of this earlier Ancred was exhausted by the begetting of his monster, for he was content to leave, almost unmolested, the terraced gardens and well-planted spinneys that had been laid out in the tradition of John Evelyn. These, maintaining their integrity, still gently led the eye of the observer towards the site of the house and had an air of blind acquiescence in its iniquities.

Intervening trees soon obliterated Troy's first view of Ancreton. In a minute or two the train paused magnanimously at the tiny station of Ancreton Halt.

'One must face these moments, of course,' Cedric muttered, and they stepped out into a flood of wintry sunshine.

There were only two people on the platform—a young man in second lieutenant's uniform and a tall girl. They were a good-looking pair and somewhat alike—blue-eyed, dark and thin. They came forward, the young man limping and using his stick.

'Oh, lud!' Cedric complained. 'Ancreds by the shoal. Greetings, you two.'

'Hallo, Cedric,' they said without much show of enthusiasm, and the girl turned quickly and cordially towards Troy.

'This is my cousin, Fenella Ancred,' Cedric explained languidly. 'And the warrior is another cousin, Paul Kentish. Miss Agatha Troy, or should it be Mrs Alleyn? *So* difficult.'

'It's splendid that you've come,' said Fenella Ancred. 'Grandfather's terribly excited and easily ten years younger. Have you got lots of luggage? If so, we'll either make two journeys or would you mind walking up the hill? We've only brought the governess-cart and Rosinante's a bit elderly.'

'Walk!' Cedric screamed faintly. 'My dear Fenella, you must be demented! Me? Rosinante (and may I say in parentheses I consider the naming of this animal an insufferable piece of whimsy), Rosinante shall bear me up the hill though it be its last conscious act.'

'I've got two suitcases and my painting gear,' said Troy, 'which is pretty heavy.'

'We'll see what can be done about it,' said Paul Kentish, eyeing Cedric with distaste. 'Come on, Fen.'

Troy's studio easel and heavy luggage had to be left at a cottage, to be sent up later in the evening by carrier, but they packed her worn hand luggage and Cedric's green shade suitcases into the governess-cart and got on top of them. The fat white pony strolled away with them down a narrow lane.

'It's a mile to the gates,' Paul Kentish said, 'and another mile up to the house. We'll get out at the gates, Fen.'

'I should like to walk,' said Troy.

'Then Cedric,' said Fenella with satisfaction, 'can drive.'

'But I'm not a horsy boy,' Cedric protested. 'The creature might sit down or turn round and bite me. Don't you think you're being rather beastly?'

'Don't be an ass,' said Fenella. 'He'll just go on walking home.'

'Who's in residence?' Cedric demanded.

'The usual,' she said. 'Mummy's coming for the weekend after this. I'm on leave for a fortnight. Otherwise, Aunt Milly and Aunt Pauline. That's Cedric's mother and Paul's mother,' Fenella explained to Troy. 'I expect you'll find us rather muddling to begin with. Aunt Pauline's Mrs Kentish and Mummy's Mrs Claude Ancred, and Aunt Millamant's Mrs Henry Ancred.'

'Henry *Irving* Ancred, don't forget,' Cedric cut in, 'deceased. My papa, you know.'

'That's all,' said Fenella, 'in our part. Of course there's Panty' (Cedric moaned), 'Caroline Able and the school in the West Wing. Aunt Pauline's helping them, you know. They're terribly short staffed. That's all.'

'All?' cried Cedric. 'You don't mean to tell me Sonia's gone?'

'No, she's there. I'd forgotten her,' said Fenella shortly.

'Well, Fenella, all I can say is you've an enviable faculty for forgetting. You'll be saying next that everyone's reconciled to Sonia.'

'Is there any point in discussing it?' said Paul Kentish very coldly.

'It's the only topic of any interest at Ancreton,' Cedric rejoined. 'Personally I find it vastly intriguing. I've been telling Mrs Alleyn all about it in the train.'

'Honestly, Cedric,' said Paul and Fenella together, 'you *are!*'

Cedric gave a crowing laugh and they drove on in an uncomfortable silence. Feeling a little desperate, Troy at last began to talk to Paul Kentish. He was a pleasant fellow, she thought, serious-minded, but friendly and ready to speak about his war service. He had been wounded in the leg during the Italian campaign and was still having treatment. Troy asked him what he was going to do when he was discharged, and was surprised to see him turn rather pink.

'As a matter of fact I rather thought—well, actually I had wondered about the police,' said Paul.

'My dear, how terrifying,' Cedric interposed.

'Paul's the only one of us,' Fenella explained, 'who really doesn't want to have anything to do with the theatre.'

'I would have liked to go on in the army,' Paul added, 'only now I'm no good for that. Perhaps, I don't know, but perhaps I'd be no good for the police either.'

'You'd better talk to my husband when he comes back,' Troy said, wondering if Alleyn would mind very much if he did.

'I say!' said Paul. 'That would be perfectly marvellous if you really mean it.'

'Well, I mean he could just tell you whether your limp would make any difference.'

'How glad I am,' Cedric remarked, 'about my duodenal ulcer! I mean I needn't even pretend I want to be brave or strenuous. No doubt I've inherited the Old Person's guts.'

'Are you going on the stage?' Troy asked Fenella.

'I expect so now the war's over. I've been a chauffeur for the duration.'

'You will play exotic roles, Fenella, and I shall design wonderful clothes for you. It would be rather fun,' Cedric went on, 'when and if I inherit Ancreton, to turn it into a frightfully exclusive theatre. The only catch in that is that Sonia might be there as the dowager baronetess, in which case she would insist on playing all the leading roles. Oh, dear, I *do* want some money so badly. What do you suppose is the best technique, Fenella? Shall I woo the Old Person or suck up to Sonia? Paul, you know all about the strategy of indirect approach. Advise me, my dear.'

'Considering you're supposed to earn about twice as much as any of the rest of us!'

'Pure legend. A pittance, I assure you.'

The white pony had sauntered into a lane that ran directly up to the gates of Ancreton, which was now displayed to its greatest advantage. A broad walk ran straight from the gates across a series of terraces, and by way of flights of steps up to a platform before the house. The carriage-drive swept away to the left and was hidden by woods. They must be an extremely rich family, Troy decided, to have kept all this going, and as if in answer to her thoughts, Fenella said: 'You wouldn't guess from here how much the flower gardens have gone back, would you?'

'Are the problem children still digging for a Freudian victory?' asked Cedric.

'They're doing a jolly good job of work,' Paul rejoined. 'All the second terrace was down in potatoes this year. You can see them up there now.' Troy had already noticed a swarm of minute figures on the second terrace.

'The potato!' Cedric murmured. 'A pregnant sublimation, I feel sure.'

'You enjoy eating them, anyway,' Fenella said bluntly.

'Here we are, Mrs Alleyn. Do you honestly feel like walking? If so, we'll go up the Middle Walk and Cedric can drive.'

They climbed out. Paul opened the elaborate and becrested iron gates, explaining that the lodge was now used as a storehouse for vegetables. Cedric, holding the reins with a great show of distaste, was borne slowly off to the left. The other three began the ascent of the terraces.

The curiously metallic sound of children's singing quavered threadily in the autumn air.

Then sing a yeo-heave ho,
Across the seas we'll go;
There's many a girl that I know well
On the banks of the Sacramento.

As they climbed the second flight of steps a woman's crisp voice could be heard, dominating the rest.

And *Down*, and *Kick*, and *Hee-ee-eeve*. Back.
And *Down*, and *Kick* and *Hee-ee-ve*.

On the second terrace some thirty little girls and boys were digging in time to their own singing. A red-haired young woman, clad in breeches and sweater, shouted the rhythmic orders. Troy was just in time to see a little boy in the back row deliberately heave a spadeful of soil down the neck of a near-by little girl. Singing shrilly, she retaliated by catching him a swinging smack across the rump with the flat of her spade.

'And *Down* and *Kick* and *Heave*. Back,' shouted the young woman, waving cheerfully to Paul and Fenella.

'Come over here!' Fenella screamed. The young woman left her charges and strode towards them. The singing continued, but with less vigour. She was extremely pretty. Fenella introduced her: Miss Caroline Able. She shook hands firmly with Troy, who noticed that the little girl, having downed the little boy, now sat on his face and had begun methodically to plaster his head with soil. In order to do this she had been obliged first to remove a curious white cap. Several of the other children, Troy noticed, wore similar caps.

'You're keeping them hard at it, aren't you, Carol?' said Fenella.

'We stop in five minutes. It's extraordinarily helpful, you know. They feel they're doing something constructive. Something socially worth while,' said Miss Able glowingly. 'And once you can get these children, especially the introverted types, to do that, you've gone quite a bit of the way.'

Fenella and Paul, who had their backs to the children, nodded gravely. The little boy, having unseated the little girl, was making a brave attempt to bite the calf of her left leg.

'How are their heads?' Paul asked solemnly. Miss Able shrugged her shoulders. 'Taking its course,' she said. 'The doctor's coming again tomorrow.'

Troy gave an involuntary exclamation, and at the same moment the little girl screamed so piercingly that her voice rang out above the singing, which instantly stopped.

'It's—perhaps you ought to look,' said Troy, and Miss Able turned in time to see the little girl attempting strenuously to kick her opponent, who nevertheless maintained his hold on her leg. 'Let go, you cow,' screamed the little girl.

'*Patricia! David!*' cried Miss Able firmly and strode towards them. The other children stopped work and listened in silence. The two principals, maintaining their hold on each other, broke into mutual accusations.

'Now, I wonder,' said Miss Able brightly, and with an air of interest, 'just what made you two feel you'd like to have a fight.' Confused recriminations followed immediately. Miss Able seemed to understand them, and, to Troy's astonishment, actually jotted down one or two notes in a little book, glancing at her watch as she did so.

'And now,' she said, still more brightly, 'you feel ever so much better. You were just angry, and you had to work it off, didn't you? But you know I can think of something that would be much better fun than fighting.'

'No, you can't,' said the little girl instantly, and turned savagely on her opponent. 'I'll kill you,' she said, and fell upon him.

'Suppose,' shouted Miss Able with determined gaiety above the shrieks of the contestants, 'we all shoulder spades and have a jolly good marching song.'

The little girl rolled clear of her opponent, scooped up a handful of earth, and flung it madly and accurately at Miss Able. The little boy and several of the other children laughed very loudly at this exploit. Miss Able, after a second's pause, joined in their laughter.

'Little devil,' said Paul. 'Honestly, Fenella, I really do think a damn good hiding—'

'No, no,' said Fenella, 'it's the method. Listen.'

The ever-jolly Miss Able was saying: 'Well, I expect I do look pretty funny, don't I? Now, come on, let's all have a good rowdy game. Twos and threes. Choose your partners.'

The children split up into pairs, and Miss Able, wiping the earth off her face, joined the three onlookers.

'How you can put up with Panty,' Paul began.

'Oh, but she really is responding, splendidly,' Miss Able interrupted. 'That's the first fight in seven and a half hours, and David began it. He's rather a bad case of maladjustment, I'm afraid. Now, Patricia,' she shouted. 'Into the middle with you. And David, you see if you can catch her. One tries as far as possible,' she explained, 'to divert the anger impulse into less emotional channels.'

They left her, briskly conducting the game, and continued their ascent. On the fourth terrace they encountered a tall and extremely good-looking woman dressed in tweeds and a felt hat, and wearing heavy gauntleted gloves.

'This is my mother,' said Paul Kentish.

Mrs Kentish greeted Troy rather uncertainly: 'You've come to paint Father, haven't you?' she said, inclining her head in the manner of a stage dowager. 'Very nice. I do hope you'll be comfortable. In these days—one can't quite'—she brightened a little—'but perhaps as an artist you won't mind rather a Bohemian—' Her voice trailed away and she turned to her son: 'Paul, *darling*,' she said richly, 'you shouldn't have walked up all those steps. Your poor leg. Fenella, dear, you shouldn't have let him.'

'It's good for my leg, Mother.'

Mrs Kentish shook her head and gazed mistily at her glowering son. 'Such a brave old boy,' she said. Her voice, which was a warm one, shook a little, and Troy saw with embarrassment that her eyes had filled with tears: 'Such an old Trojan,' she murmured, 'Isn't he, Fenella?'

Fenella laughed uncomfortably and Paul hastily backed away. 'Where are you off to?' he asked loudly.

'To remind Miss Able it's time to come in. Those poor children work so hard. I can't feel—however. I'm afraid I'm rather old-fashioned, Mrs Alleyn. I still feel a mother knows best.'

'Well, but Mother,' Paul objected, 'something had to be done about Panty, didn't it? I mean, she really was pretty frightful.'

'Poor old Panty!' said Mrs Kentish bitterly.

'We'd better move on, Aunt Pauline,' Fenella said. 'Cedric is driving up. He won't do anything about unloading if I know him.'

'Cedric!' Mrs Kentish repeated. 'T'uh!'

She smiled rather grandly at Troy and left them.

'My mother,' Paul said uncomfortably, 'gets in a bit of a flap about things. Doesn't she, Fen?'

'Actually,' said Fenella, 'they all do. That generation, I mean. Daddy rather wallows in emotion and Aunt Dessy's a snorter at it. They get it from Grandfather, don't you think?'

'All except Thomas.'

'Yes, all except Thomas. Don't you think,' Fenella asked Troy, 'that if one generation comes in rather hot and strong emotionally, the next generation swings very much the other way? Paul and I are as hard as nails, aren't we, Paul?'

Troy turned to the young man. He was staring fixedly at his cousin. His dark brows were knitted and his lips were pressed together. He looked preternaturally solemn and did not answer Fenella. 'Why,' thought Troy, 'he's in love with her.'

❊ ❊ ❊

The interior of Ancreton amply sustained the promise of its monstrous facade. Troy was to learn that 'great' was the stock adjective at Ancreton. There was the Great West Spinney, the

Great Gallery and the Great Tower. Having crossed the Great Drawbridge over the now dry and cultivated moat, Troy, Fenella, and Paul entered the Great Hall.

Here the tireless ingenuity of the architect had flirted with a number of Elizabethan conceits. There was a plethora of fancy carving, a display of stained-glass windows bearing the Ancred arms, and a number of presumably collateral quarterings. Between these romped occasional mythical animals, and, when mythology and heraldry had run short, the Church had not been forgotten, for crosslets-ancred stood cheek-by-jowl in mild confusion with the keys of St Peter and the Cross of St John of Jerusalem.

Across the back of the hall, facing the entrance, ran a minstrels' gallery, energetically chiselled and hung at inter-vals with banners. Beneath this, on a wall whose surface was a mass of scrolls and bosses, the portrait, Fenella explained, was to hang. By day, as Troy at once noticed, it would be chequered all over with the reflected colours of a stained-glass heraldry and would take on the aspect of a jig-saw puzzle. By night, according to Paul, it would be floodlit by four lamps specially installed under the gallery.

There were a good many portraits already in the hall, and Troy's attention was caught by an enormous canvas above the fireplace depicting a nautical Ancred of the eighteenth century, who pointed his cutlass at a streak of forked lightning with an air of having made it himself. Underneath this work, in a huge armchair, warming himself at the fire, was Cedric.

'People are seeing about the luggage,' he said, struggling to his feet, 'and one of the minor ancients has led away the horse. Someone has carried dearest Mrs Alleyn's paints up to her inaccessible eyrie. *Do* sit down, Mrs Alleyn. You must be madly exhausted. My Mama is on her way. The Old Person's entrance is timed for eight-thirty. We have a nice long time in which to relax. The Ancient of Days, at my suggestion, is about to serve drinks. In the name of my ridiculous family, in fact, welcome to Katzenjammer Castle.'

'Would you like to see your room first?' asked Fenella.

'Let me warn you,' Cedric added, 'that the visit will entail another arduous climb and a long tramp. Where have they put her, Fenella?'

'The *Siddons* room.'

'I couldn't sympathize more deeply, but of course the choice is appropriate. A steel engraving of that abnormally muscular actress in the role of Lady Macbeth hangs over the washhand-stand, doesn't it, Fenella? I'm in the *Garrick*, which is comparatively lively, especially in the rat season. Here comes the Ancient of Days. *Do* have a stirrup-cup before you set out on your polar expedition.'

An extremely old man-servant was coming across the hall with a tray of drinks. 'Barker,' said Cedric faintly. 'You are welcome as flowers in spring.'

'Thank you, Mr Cedric,' said the old man. 'Sir Henry's compliments, Miss Fenella, and he hopes to have the pleasure of joining you at dinner. Sir Henry hopes Mrs Alleyn has had a pleasant journey.'

Troy said that she had, and wondered if she should return a formal message. Cedric, with the nearest approach to energy that he had yet displayed, began to mix drinks. 'There is one department of Katzenjammer Castle to which one can find *no* objection, and that is the cellar,' he said 'Thank you, Barker, from my heart. Ganymede himself couldn't foot it more featly.'

'I must say, Cedric,' Paul muttered when the old butler had gone, 'that I don't think your line of comedy with Barker is screamingly funny.'

'Dear Paul! Don't you? I'm completely shattered.'

'Well, he's old,' said Fenella quickly, 'and he's a great friend.'

Cedric darted an extraordinarily malicious glance at his cousins. 'How very feudal,' he said. '*Noblesse oblige.* Dear me!'

At this juncture, rather to Troy's relief, a stout smiling woman came in from one of the side doors. Behind her, Troy caught a glimpse of a vast formal drawing-room.

'This is my Mama,' Cedric explained, faintly waving his hand.

Mrs Henry Ancred was a firmly built white-skinned woman. Her faded hair was scrupulously groomed into a rather wig-like coiffure. She looked, Troy thought, a little as if she managed some quiet but extremely expensive boarding-house or perhaps a school. Her voice was unusually deep, and her hands and feet unusually large. Unlike her son, she had a wide mouth, but there was a resemblance to Cedric about the eyes and chin. She wore a sensible blouse, a cardigan, and a dark skirt, and she shook hands heartily with Troy. A capable woman.

'So glad you've decided to come,' she said. 'My father-in-law's quite excited. It will take him out of himself and fill in his day nicely.'

Cedric gave a little shriek: 'Milly, *darling!*' he cried. 'How—you can!' He made an agonized face at Troy.

'Have I said something I shouldn't?' asked his mother. 'So like me!' And she laughed heartily.

'Of course you haven't,' Troy said hurriedly, ignoring Cedric. 'I only hope the sittings won't tire Sir Henry.'

'Oh, he'll tell you at once if he's tired,' Millamant Ancred assured her, and Troy had an unpleasant picture of a canvas six by four feet, to be completed in a fortnight, with a sitter who had no hesitation in telling her when he felt tired.

'Well, anyway,' Cedric cried shrilly. 'Drinks!'

They sat round the fire, Paul and Fenella on a sofa, Troy opposite them, and Millamant Ancred, squarely, on a high chair. Cedric pulled a humpty up to his mother, curled himself on it, and rested an arm on her knees. Paul and Fenella glanced at him with ill-concealed distaste.

'What have you been doing, dear?' Millamant asked her son, and put her square white hand on his shoulder.

'Such a lot of tiresome jobs,' he sighed, rubbing his cheek on the hand. 'Tell us what's going to happen here. I want something gay and exciting. A party for Mrs Alleyn. Please!

You'd like a party, wouldn't you?' he persisted, appealing to Troy. 'Say you would.'

'But I've come to work,' said Troy, and because he made her feel uncomfortable she spoke abruptly. 'Damn!' she thought. 'Even that sounds as if I expected her to take him seriously.'

But Millamant laughed indulgently. 'Mrs Alleyn will be with us for The Birthday,' she said, 'and so will you, dear, if you really can stay for ten days. Can you?'

'Oh, yes,' he said fretfully. 'The office-place is being tatted up. I've brought my dreary work with me. But The Birthday! How abysmally depressing! Darling Milly, I don't think, really, that I can face another Birthday.'

'Don't be naughty,' said Millamant in her gruff voice.

'Let's have another drink,' said Paul loudly.

'Is somebody talking about drink?' cried a disembodied voice in the minstrels' gallery. 'Goody! Goody! Goody!'

'Oh, God!' Cedric whispered. 'Sonia!'

❀ ❀ ❀

It had grown dark in the hall, and Troy's first impression of Miss Sonia Orrincourt was of a whitish apparition that fluttered down the stairs from the far side of the gallery. Her progress was accompanied by a number of chirruping noises. As she reached the hall and crossed it, Troy saw that she wore a garment which even in the second act of a musical extravaganza would still have been remarkable. Troy supposed it was a negligée.

'Well, for heaven's sake,' squeaked Miss Orrincourt, 'look who's here! Ceddie!' She held out both her hands and Cedric took them.

'You look too marvellous, Sonia,' he cried. 'Where did it come from?'

'Darling, it's a million years old. Oh, pardon me,' said Miss Orrincourt, inclining towards Troy, 'I didn't see—'

Millamant stonily introduced her. Fenella and Paul, having moved away from the sofa, Miss Orrincourt sank into it. She extended her arms and wriggled her fingers. 'Quick! Quick! Quick!' she cried babyishly. 'Sonia wants a d'ink.'

Her hair was almost white. It fell in a fringe across her forehead and in a silk curtain to her shoulders, and reminded Troy vaguely of the inside of an aquarium. Her eyes were as round as saucers, with curving black lashes. When she smiled, her short upper lip flattened, the corners of her mouth turned down, and the shadow of grooves-to-come ran away to her chin. Her skin was white and thick like the petals of a camellia. She was a startling young woman to look at, and she made Troy feel exceedingly dumb. 'But she'd probably be pretty good to paint in the nude,' she reflected. 'I wonder if she's ever been a model. She looks like it.'

Miss Orrincourt and Cedric were conducting an extraordinarily unreal little conversation. Fenella and Paul had moved away, and Troy was left with Millamant Ancred, who began to talk about the difficulties of housekeeping. As she talked, she stitched at an enormous piece of embroidery, which hypnotized Troy by its monstrous colour scheme and tortuous design. Intricate worms and scrolls strangled each other in Millamant's fancy work. No area was left undecorated, no motive was uninterrupted. At times she would pause and eye it with complacency. Her voice was monotonous.

'I suppose I'm lucky,' she said. 'I've got a cook and five maids and Barker, but they're all very old, and have been collected from different branches of the family. My sister-in-law, Pauline, Mrs Claude Ancred, you know, gave up her own house in the evacuation time and has recently joined us with two of her maids. Desdemona did the same thing, and she makes Ancreton her headquarters now. She brought her old Nanny. Barker and the others have always been with us. But even with the West Wing turned into a school it's difficult. In the old days of course,' said Millamant with a certain air of complacency, 'there was a swarm.'

'Do they get on together?' Troy asked vaguely. She was watching Cedric and Miss Orrincourt. Evidently he had decided to adopt ingratiating tactics, and a lively but completely synthetic flirtation had developed. They whispered together.

'Oh, no,' Millamant was saying. 'They fight.' And most unexpectedly she added: 'Like master like man, they say, don't they?' Troy looked at her. She was smiling broadly and blankly. It is a characteristic of these people, Troy reflected, that they constantly make remarks to which there is no answer.

Pauline Ancred came in and joined her son and Fenella. She did this with a certain air of determination, and the smile she gave Fenella was a dismissal. 'Darling,' she said to Paul, 'I've been looking for you.' Fenella at once moved away. Pauline, using a gesture that was Congrevian in its accomplishment, raised a pair of lorgnettes and stared through them at Miss Orrincourt, who now reclined at full length on the sofa. Cedric was perched on the arm at her feet.

'I'll get you a chair, Mother,' said Paul hastily.

'Thank you, dear,' she said, exchanging a glance with her sister-in-law. 'I should like to sit down. No, *please*, Mrs Alleyn, don't move. So sweet of you. Thank you, Paul.'

'Noddy and I,' said Miss Orrincourt brightly, 'have been having such fun. We've been looking at some of that old jewellery.' She stretched her arms above her head and yawned delicately.

'Noddy?' Troy wondered. 'But who is Noddy?' Miss Orrincourt's remark was followed by a rather deadly little pause. 'He's all burnt up about having his picture taken,' Miss Orrincourt added. 'Isn't it killing?'

Pauline Ancred, with a dignified shifting of her torso, brought her sister-in-law into her field of vision. 'Have you seen Papa this afternoon, Millamant?' she asked, not quite cordially, but with an air of joining forces against a common enemy.

'I went up as usual at four o'clock,' Millamant rejoined, 'to see if there was anything I could do for him.' She glanced at Miss Orrincourt. 'He was engaged, however.'

'T'uh!' said Pauline lightly, and she began to revolve her thumbs one around the other. Millamant gave the merest sketch of a significant laugh and turned to Troy.

'We don't quite know,' she said cheerfully, 'if Thomas explained about my father-in-law's portrait. He wishes to be painted in his own little theatre here. The backcloth has been hung and Paul knows about the lights. Papa would like to begin at eleven tomorrow morning, and if he is feeling up to it he will sit for an hour every morning and afternoon.'

'I thought,' said Miss Orrincourt, 'it would be ever so thrilling if Noddy was on a horse in the picture.'

'Sir Henry,' said Millamant, without looking at her, 'will, of course, have decided on the pose.'

'But Aunt Milly,' said Paul, very red in the face, 'Mrs Alleyn might like—I mean—don't you think—'

'Yes, Aunt Milly,' said Fenella.

'Yes, indeed, Milly,' said Cedric. 'I *so* agree. Please, *please* Milly and Aunt Pauline, and please Sonia, angel, *do* consider that Mrs Alleyn is the one to—oh, my goodness,' Cedric implored them, 'pray do consider.'

'I shall be very interested,' said Troy, 'to hear about Sir Henry's plans.'

'That,' said Pauline, 'will be very nice. I forgot to tell you, Millamant, that I heard from Dessy. She's coming for The Birthday.'

'I'm glad you let me know,' said Millamant, looking rather put out.

'And so's Mummy, Aunt Milly,' said Fenella. 'I forgot to say.'

'Well,' said Millamant, with a short laugh, 'I *am* learning about things, aren't I?'

'Jenetta coming? Fancy!' said Pauline. 'It must be two years since Jenetta was at Ancreton. I hope she'll be able to put up with our rough and ready ways.'

'Considering she's been living in a two-roomed flat,' Fenella began rather hotly and checked herself. 'She asked me to say she hoped it wouldn't be too many.'

'I'll move out of *Bernhardt* into *Bracegirdle*,' Pauline offered. 'Of course.'

'You'll do nothing of the sort, Pauline,' said Millamant. '*Bracegirdle* is piercingly cold, the ceiling leaks, and there are rats. Desdemona complained bitterly about the rats last time she was here. I asked Barker to lay poison for them, but he's lost the poison. Until he finds it, *Bracegirdle* is uninhabitable.'

'Mummy could share *Duse* with me,' said Fenella quickly. 'We'd love it and it'd save fires.'

'Oh, we couldn't dream of *that*,' said Pauline and Millamant together.

'Mrs Alleyn,' said Fenella loudly, 'I'm going up to change. Would you like to see your room?'

'Thank you,' said Troy, trying not to sound too eager. 'Thank you, I would.'

❁ ❁ ❁

Having climbed the stairs and walked with a completely silent Fenella down an interminable picture gallery and two long passages, followed by a break-neck ascent up a winding stair, Troy found herself at a door upon which hung a wooden plaque bearing the word '*Siddons*.' Fenella opened the door, and Troy was pleasantly welcomed by the reflection of leaping flames on white painted walls. White damask curtains with small garlands, a sheepskin rug, a low bed, and there, above a Victorian wash-stand, sure enough, hung Mrs Siddons. Troy's painting gear was stacked in a corner.

'What a nice room,' said Troy.

'I'm glad you like it,' said Fenella in a suppressed voice. Troy saw with astonishment that she was in a rage.

'I apologize,' said Fenella shakily, 'for my beastly family.'

'Hallo,' said Troy, 'what's all this?'

'As if they weren't damned lucky to get you! As if they wouldn't still be damned lucky if you decided to paint Grandpa standing on his head with garlic growing out of the

soles of his boots. It's *such cheek*. Even that frightful twirp
Cedric was ashamed.'

'Good Lord!' said Troy 'That's nothing unusual. You've
no conception how funny people can be about portraits.'

'I hate them! And you heard how catty they were about
Mummy coming. I do think old women are *foul*. And that
bitch Sonia lying there lapping it all up. How they can, in
front of her! Paul and I were so ashamed.'

Fenella stamped, dropped on her knees in front of the
fire and burst into tears. 'I'm sorry,' she stammered. 'I'm
worse than they are, but I'm so sick of it all. I wish I hadn't
come to Ancreton. I loathe Ancreton. If you only knew what
it's like.'

'Look here,' Troy said gently, 'are you sure you want to
talk to me like this?'

'I know it's frightful, but I can't help it. How would you
feel if *your* grandfather brought a loathsome blonde into the
house? How would you feel?'

Troy had a momentary vision of her grandfather, now
deceased. He had been an austere and somewhat finicky don.

'Everybody's laughing at him,' Fenella sobbed. 'And I
used to like him so much. Now he's just *silly*. A silly amorous
old man. He behaves like that himself and then when I—
when I went to—it doesn't matter. I'm terribly sorry. It's
awful, boring you like this.'

Troy sat on a low chair by the fire and looked thoughtfully at Fenella. The child really is upset, she thought, and
realized that already she had begun to question the authenticity of the Ancreds' emotions. She said: 'You needn't think
it's awful, and you're not boring me. Only don't say things
you'll feel inclined to kick yourself for when you've got under
way again.'

'All right.' Fenella got to her feet. She had the fortunate
knack, Troy noticed, of looking charming when she cried.
She now tossed her head, bit her lips, and gained mastery
of herself. 'She'll make a good actress,' Troy thought, and

instantly checked herself. 'Because,' she thought, 'the child manages to be so prettily distressed, why should I jump to the conclusion that she's not as distressed as she seems? I'm not sympathetic enough.' She touched Fenella's arm, and although it was quite foreign to her habit, returned the squeeze Fenella instantly gave to her hand.

'Come,' said Troy, 'I thought you said this afternoon that your generation of Ancreds was as hard as nails.'

'Well, we try,' Fenella said. 'It's only because you're so nice that I let go. I won't again.'

'Help!' Troy thought, and said aloud: 'I'm not much use really, I'm afraid. My husband says I shy away from emotion like a nervous mare. But let off steam if you want to.'

Fenella said soberly: 'This'll do for a bit, I expect. You're an angel. Dinner's at half-past eight. You'll hear a warning gong.' She turned at the door. 'All the same,' she said, 'there's something pretty ghastly going on at Ancreton just now. You'll see.'

With an inherited instinct for a good exit line, Fenella stepped backwards and gracefully closed the door.

CHAPTER FOUR

Sir Henry

IN HER AGITATION FENELLA had neglected to give Troy the usual hostesses' tips on internal topography. Troy wondered if the nearest bathroom was at the top of another tower or at the end of some interminable corridor. Impossible to tug the embroidered bell-pull and cause one of those aged maids to climb the stairs! She decided to give up her bath in favour of Mrs Siddons, the wash-stand and a Victorian can of warm water which had been left beside it.

She had an hour before dinner. It was pleasant, after the severely rationed fires of Tatler's End, to dress leisurely before this sumptuous blaze. She made the most of it, turning over in her mind the events of the day and sorting out her impressions of the Ancreds. Queer Thomas, she decided, was, so far, the best of the bunch, though the two young things were pleasant enough. Was there an understanding between them and had Sir Henry objected? Was that the reason for Fenella's outburst? For the rest: Pauline appeared to be suffering from a general sense of personal affront, Millamant was an unknown quantity, while her Cedric was frankly awful. And then, Sonia! Troy giggled. Sonia really was a bit thick.

Somewhere outside in the cold, a deep-toned clock struck eight. The fire had died down. She might as well begin her journey to the hall. Down the winding stair she went, wondering whose room lay beyond a door on the landing. Troy had no sense of direction. When she reached the first long corridor she couldn't for the life of her remember whether she should turn left or right. A perspective of dark crimson carpet stretched away on each hand, and at intervals the corridor was lit by pseudo-antique candelabra. 'Oh, well,' thought Troy and turned to the right. She passed four doors and read their legends: *'Duse'* (that was Fenella's room), *'Bernhardt'* (Pauline's), *'Terry,' 'Lady Bancroft,'* and, near the end of the passage, the despised *'Bracegirdle.'* Troy did not remember seeing any of these names on her way up to her tower. 'Blast!' she thought, 'I've gone wrong.' But she went on uncertainly. The corridor led at right-angles into another, at the far end of which she saw the foot of a flight of stairs like those of her own tower. Poor Troy was certain that she had looked down just such a vista on her way up. 'But I suppose,' she thought, 'it must have been its opposite number. From outside, the damn place looked as if it was built round a sort of quadrangle, with a tower at the middle and ends of each wing. In that case, if I keep on turning left, oughtn't I to come back to the picture gallery?'

As she hesitated, a door near the foot of the stairs opened slightly, and a magnificent cat walked out into the passage.

He was white, with a tabby saddle on his back, long haired and amber eyed. He paused and stared at Troy. Then, wafting his tail slightly, he paced slowly towards her. She stooped and waited for him. After some deliberation he approached, examined her hand, bestowed upon it a brief cold thrust of his nose, and continued on his way, walking in the centre of the crimson carpet and still elegantly wafting his tail.

'And one other thing,' said a shrill voice beyond the open door, 'if you think I'm going to hang round here like a bloody extra with the family handing me out the bird in fourteen different positions you've got another think coming.'

A deep voice rumbled unintelligibly.

'I know all about that, and it makes no difference. Nobody's going to tell me I lack refinement and get away with it. They treat me as if I had one of those things in the strip ads. I kept my temper down there because I wasn't going to let them see I minded. What do they think they are? My God, do they think it's any catch living in a mausoleum with a couple of old tats and a kid that ought to be labelled "Crazy Gang"?'

Again the expostulatory rumble.

'I know, I know, I know. It's so merry and bright in this dump it's a wonder we don't all die of laughing. If you're as crazy as all that about me, you ought to put me in a position where I'd keep my self-respect…You owe it to me…After all I've done for you. I'm just miserable…And when I get like this, I'm warning you, Noddy, look out.' The door opened a little further.

Troy, who had stood transfixed, picked up her skirts, turned back on her tracks, and fairly ran away down the long corridor.

❋ ❋ ❋

This time she reached the gallery and went downstairs. In the hall she encountered Barker, who showed her into an enormous drawing-room which looked, she thought, as if it was the setting for a scene in 'Victoria Regina.' Crimson, white, and gold were the predominant colours, damask and velvet the prevailing textures. Vast canvases by Leader and MacWhirter occupied the walls. On each occasional table or cabinet stood a silver-framed photograph of Royalty or Drama. There were three of Sir Henry at different stages of his career, and there was one of Sir Henry in Court dress. In this last portrait, the customary air of a man who can't help feeling he looks a bit of an ass was completely absent, and for a moment Troy thought Sir Henry had been taken in yet another of his professional roles. The unmistakable authenticity of his Windsor coat undeceived her. 'Golly,' she thought, staring at the photograph, 'it's a good head and no mistake.'

She began a tour of the room and found much to entertain her. Under the glass lid of a curio table were set out a number of orders, miniatures and decorations, several *objets d'art*, a signed programme from a command performance, and, surprisingly, a small book of antique style, bound in half-calf and heavily tooled. Troy was one of those people who, when they see a book lying apart, must handle it. The lid was unlocked. She raised it and opened the little book. The title was much faded, and Troy stooped to make it out.

The Antient Arte of the Embalming of Corpfes [she read]. To which is added a Difcourfe on the Concoction of Fluids for the Purpofe of Preferving Dead Bodies.

By William Hurfte, Profeffor of Phyfic, London.

Printed by Robert White for John Crampe at the Sign of the Three Bibles in St Paul's Churchyard. 1678.

It was horribly explicit. Here, in the first chapter, were various recipes 'For the Confumation of the Arte of Preferving the Dead in perfect Verifimilitude of Life. It will be remarked,' the author continued, 'that in fpite of their diverfity the chimical of Arfenic is Common to All.' There was a particularly macabre passage on 'The ufe of Cofmetics to Difguife the ghaftly Pallor of Death.'

'But what sort of mind,' Troy wondered, 'could picture with equanimity, even with pleasure, these manipulations upon the body from which it must some day, perhaps soon, be parted?' And she wondered if Sir Henry Ancred had read this book and if he had no imagination or too much. 'And why,' she thought, 'do I go on reading this horrid little book?'

She heard a voice in the hall, and with an illogical feeling of guilt hurriedly closed the book and the glass lid. Millamant came in, wearing a tidy but nondescript evening dress.

'I've been exploring,' Troy said.

'Exploring?' Millamant repeated with her vague laugh.

'That grisly little book in the case. I can't resist a book and I'm afraid I opened the case. I do hope it's allowed.'

'Oh,' said Millamant. 'Yes, of course.' She glanced at the case. 'What book is it?'

'It's about embalming, of all things. It's very old. I should think it might be rather valuable.'

'Perhaps,' said Millamant, 'that's why Miss Orrincourt was so interested in it.'

She moved to the fireplace, looking smugly resentful.

'Miss Orrincourt?' Troy repeated.

'I found her reading a small book when I came in the other day. She put it in the case and dropped the lid. Such a bang! It's a wonder it didn't break, really. I suppose it must have been that book, mustn't it?'

'Yes,' said Troy, hurriedly rearranging her already chaotic ideas of Miss Sonia Orrincourt. 'I suppose it must.'

'Papa,' said Millamant, 'is not quite at his best this evening but he's coming down. On his bad days he dines in his own rooms.'

'I hope,' said Troy, 'that the sittings won't tire him too much.'

'Well, he's so looking forward to them that I'm sure he'll try to keep them up. He's really been much better lately, only sometimes,' said Millamant ambiguously, 'he gets a little upset. He's very highly strung and sensitive, you know I always think that all the Ancreds are like that. Except Thomas. My poor Cedric, unfortunately, has inherited their temperament.'

Troy had nothing to say to this, and was relieved when Paul Kentish and his mother came in, followed in a moment by Fenella. Barker brought a tray with sherry. Presently an extraordinarily ominous gong sounded in the hall.

'Did anyone see Cedric?' asked his mother. 'I do hope he's not going to be late.'

'He was still in his bath when I tried to get in ten minutes ago,' said Paul.

'Oh, dear,' said Millamant.

Miss Orrincourt, amazingly dressed, and looking at once sulky, triumphant and defiant, drifted into the room. Troy heard a stifled exclamation behind her, and turned to see the assembled Ancreds with their gaze riveted to Miss Orrincourt's bosom.

It was adorned with a large diamond star.

'Milly,' Pauline muttered.

'Do you see what I see?' Millamant replied with a faint hiss.

Miss Orrincourt moved to the fire and laid one arm along the mantelpiece. 'I hope Noddy's not going to be late,' she said. 'I'm starving.' She looked critically at her crimson nails and touched the diamond star. 'I'd like a drink,' she said.

Nobody made any response to this statement, though Paul uncomfortably cleared his throat. The tap of a stick sounded in the hall.

'Here *is* Papa,' said Pauline nervously, and they all moved slightly. Really, thought Troy, they might be waiting to dine with some minor royalty. There was precisely the same air of wary expectation.

Barker opened the door, and the original of all the photographs walked slowly into the room, followed by the white cat.

❀ ❀ ❀

The first thing to be said about Sir Henry Ancred was that he filled his role with almost embarrassing virtuosity. He was unbelievably handsome. His hair was silver, his eyes, under heavy brows, were fiercely blue. His nose was ducal in its prominence. Beneath it sprouted a fine snowy moustache, brushed up to lend accent to his actor's mouth. His chin jutted out squarely and was adorned with an ambassado-rial tuft. He looked as if he had been specially designed for exhibition. He wore a velvet dinner-jacket, an old-fashioned collar, a wide cravat and a monocle on a broad ribbon. You could hardly believe, Troy thought, that he was true. He came in slowly, using a black and silver stick, but not leaning on it overmuch. It was, Troy felt, more of an adjunct than an aid. He was exceeding tall and still upright.

'Mrs Alleyn, Papa,' said Pauline.

'Ah,' said Sir Henry.

Troy went to meet him. 'Restraining myself,' as she after-wards told Alleyn, 'from curtsying, but with difficulty.'

'So this is our distinguished painter?' said Sir Henry, taking her hand. 'I am delighted.'

He kept her hand in his and looked down at her. Behind him, Troy saw in fancy a young Henry Ancred bending his gaze upon the women in his heyday and imagined how pleasurably they must have melted before it. 'Delighted,' he repeated, and his voice underlined adroitly his pleasure not only in her arrival but in her looks. 'Hold your horses, chaps,' thought Troy and removed her hand. 'I hope you continue of that mind,' she said politely.

Sir Henry bowed. 'I believe I shall,' he said. 'I believe I shall.' She was to learn that he had a habit of repeating himself.

Paul had moved a chair forward. Sir Henry sat in it facing the fire, with the guest and family disposed in arcs on either side of him.

He crossed his knees and rested his left forearm along the arm of his chair, letting his beautifully kept hand dangle elegantly. It was a sort of Charles II pose, and, in lieu of the traditional spaniel, the white cat leapt gracefully on his lap, kneaded it briefly and reclined there.

'Ah, Carabbas!' said Sir Henry, and stroked it, looking graciously awhile upon his family and guest. 'This is pleasant,' he said, including them in a beautiful gesture. For a moment his gaze rested on Miss Orrincourt's bosom. 'Charming,' he said. 'A conversation piece. Ah! A glass of sherry.'

Paul and Fenella dispensed the sherry, which was extremely good. Rather elaborate conversation was made, Sir Henry conducting it with the air of giving an audition. 'But I thought,' he said, 'that Cedric was to join us. Didn't you tell me, Millamant—'

'I'm so sorry he's late, Papa,' said Millamant. 'He had an important letter to write, I know. I think perhaps he didn't hear the gong.'

'Indeed? Where have you put him?'

'In *Garrick*, Papa.'

'Then he certainly must have heard the gong.'

Barker came in and announced dinner.

'We shall not, I think, wait for Cedric,' Sir Henry continued. He removed the cat, Carabbas, from his knees and rose. His family rose with him. 'Mrs Alleyn, may I have the pleasure of taking you in?' he said.

'It's a pity,' Troy thought as she took the arm he curved for her, 'that there isn't an orchestra.' And as if she had recaptured the lines from some drawing-room comedy of her childhood, she made processional conversation as they moved towards the door. Before they reached it, however, there was a sound of running footsteps in the hall. Cedric, flushed with exertion and wearing a white flower in his dinner-jacket, darted into the room.

'Dearest Grandpapa,' he cried, waving his hands, 'I creep, I grovel. So sorry, truly. Couldn't be more contrite. Find me some sackcloth and ashes somebody, quickly.'

'Good evening, Cedric,' said Sir Henry icily. 'You must make your apologies to Mrs Alleyn, who will perhaps be very kind and forgive you.'

Troy smiled like a duchess at Cedric and inwardly grinned like a Cheshire cat at herself.

'Too heavenly of you,' said Cedric quickly. He slipped in behind them. The procession had splayed out a little on his entrance. He came face to face with Miss Orrincourt.

Troy heard him give a curious, half-articulate exclamation. It sounded involuntary and unaffected. This was so unusual from Cedric that Troy turned to look at him. His small mouth was open. His pale eyes stared blankly at the diamond star on Miss Orrincourt's bosom, and then turned incredulously from one member of his family to another.

'But'—he stammered—'but, I say—I say.'

'Cedric,' whispered his mother.

'Cedric,' said his grandfather imperatively.

But Cedric, still speaking in that strangely natural voice, pointed a white finger at the diamond star and said loudly: 'But, my God, it's Great-Great-Grandmama Ancred's sunburst!'

'Nice, isn't it?' said Miss Orrincourt equally loudly. 'I'm ever so thrilled.'

'In these unhappy times, alas,' said Sir Henry blandly, arming Troy through the door, 'one may not make those gestures with which one would wish to honour a distinguished visitor! "A poor small banquet," as old Capulet had it. Shall we go in?'

❋ ❋ ❋

The poor small banquet was, if nothing else, a tribute to the zeal of Sir Henry's admirers in the Dominions and the United States of America. Troy had not seen its like for years. He himself, she noticed, ate a mess of something that had been put through a sieve. Conversation was general, innocuous, and sounded a little as if it had been carefully memorized beforehand. It was difficult not to look at Miss Orrincourt's diamonds. They were a sort of visual *faux pas* which no amount of blameless small-talk could shout down. Troy observed that the Ancreds themselves constantly darted furtive glances at them. Sir Henry continued bland, urbane, and, to Troy, excessively gracious. She found his compliments, which were adroit, rather hard to counter. He spoke of her work and asked if she had done a self-portrait. 'Only in my student days when I couldn't afford a model,' said Troy. 'But that's very naughty of you,' he said. 'It is now that you should give us the perfect painting of the perfect subject.'

'Crikey!' thought Troy.

They drank Rudesheimer. When Barker hovered beside him, Sir Henry, announcing that it was a special occasion, said he would take half a glass. Millamant and Pauline looked anxiously at him.

'Papa, darling,' said Pauline. 'Do you think —?' And Millamant murmured: 'Yes, Papa. *Do* you think—?'

'Do I think what?' he replied, glaring at them.

'Wine,' they murmured disjointedly. 'Dr Withers…not really advisable…however.'

'Fill it up, Barker,' Sir Henry commanded loudly, 'fill it up.' Troy heard Pauline and Millamant sigh windily.

Dinner proceeded with circumspection but uneasily. Paul and Fenella were silent. Cedric, on Troy's right hand, conversed in feverish spasms with anybody who would listen to him. Sir Henry's flow of compliments continued unabated through three courses, and to Troy's dismay, Miss Orrincourt began to show signs of marked hostility. She was on Sir Henry's left, with Paul on her other side. She began an extremely grand conversation with Paul, and though he responded with every sign of discomfort she lowered her voice, cast significant glances at him, and laughed immoderately at his monosyllabic replies. Troy, who was beginning to find her host very heavy weather indeed, seized an opportunity to speak to Cedric.

'Noddy,' said Miss Orrincourt at once, 'what are we going to do tomorrow?'

'Do?' he repeated, and after a moment's hesitation became playful. 'What does a little girl want to do?'

Miss Orrincourt stretched her arms above her head. 'She wants things to *happen*!' she cried ecstatically, 'Lovely things.'

'Well, if she's very, *very* good perhaps we'll let her have a tiny peep at a great big picture.'

Troy heard this with dismay.

'What else?' Miss Orrincourt persisted babyishly but with an extremely unenthusiastic glance at Troy.

'We'll see,' said Sir Henry uneasily.

'But Noddy—'

'Mrs Alleyn,' said Millamant from the foot of the table, 'shall we—?'

And she marshalled her ladies out of the dining-room.

The rest of the evening passed uneventfully. Sir Henry led Troy through the pages of three albums of theatrical photographs. This she rather enjoyed. It was strange, she thought, to see how the fashion in Elizabethan garments changed in the world of theatre. Here was a young Victorian Henry Ancred very much be-pointed, be-ruffed, encased and furbished, in a perfect welter of velvet, ribbon and leather; here a modern elderly Henry Ancred in a stylized and simplified costume that had apparently been made of painted scenic canvas. Yet both were the Duke of Buckingham.

Miss Orrincourt joined a little fretfully in this pastime. Perched on the arm of Sir Henry's chair and disseminating an aura of black market scent, she giggled tactlessly over the earlier photographs and yawned over the later ones. 'My dear,' she ejaculated, 'look at you! You've got everything on but the kitchen sink!' This was in reference to a picture of Sir Henry as Richard II. Cedric tittered and immediately looked frightened. Pauline said: 'I must say, Papa, I don't think anyone else has ever approached your flair for exactly the right costume.'

'My dear,' her father rejoined, 'it's the way you wear 'em.' He patted Miss Orrincourt's hand. 'You do very well, my child,' he said, 'in your easy modern dresses. How would you manage if, like Ellen Terry, you had two feet of heavy velvet in front of you on the stage and were asked to move like a queen down a flight of stairs? You'd fall on your nice little nose.'

He was obviously a vain man. It was extraordinary, Troy thought, that he remained unmoved by Miss Orrincourt's lack of reverence, and remembering Thomas's remark about

David and Abishag the Shunammite, Troy was forced to the disagreeable conclusion that Sir Henry was in his dotage about Miss Orrincourt.

At ten o'clock a grog-tray was brought in. Sir Henry drank barley water, suffered the women of his family to kiss him goodnight, nodded to Paul and Cedric, and, to her intense embarrassment, kissed Troy's hand. '*À demain*,' he said in his deepest voice. 'We meet at eleven. I am fortunate.'

He made a magnificent exit, and ten minutes later, Miss Orrincourt, yawning extensively, also retired.

Her disappearance was the signal for an outbreak among the Ancreds.

'Honestly, Milly! Honestly, Aunt Pauline. Can we believe our *eyes*!' cried Cedric. 'The Sunburst! I mean *actually*!'

'Well, Millamant,' said Pauline, 'I now see for myself how things stand at Ancreton.'

'You wouldn't believe me when I told you, Pauline,' Millamant rejoined. 'You've been here a month, but you wouldn't—'

'Has he *given* it to her, will somebody tell me?' Cedric demanded.

'He can't,' said Pauline. 'He can't. And what's more, I don't believe he would. Unless—' She stopped short and turned to Paul. 'If he's given it to her,' she said, 'he's going to marry her. That's all.'

Poor Troy, who had been making completely ineffectual efforts to go, seized upon the silence that followed Pauline's announcement to murmur: 'If I may, I think I shall—'

'*Dear* Mrs Alleyn,' said Cedric, 'I implore you not to be tactful. Do stay and listen.'

'I don't see,' Paul began, 'why poor Mrs Alleyn should be inflicted—'

'She knows,' said Fenella. 'I'm afraid I've already told her, Paul.'

Pauline suddenly made a gracious dive at Troy. 'Isn't it disturbing?' she said with an air of drawing Troy into her confidence. 'You see how things are? Really, it's too naughty of

Papa. We're all so dreadfully worried. It's not what's happening so much as what might happen that terrifies one. And now the Sunburst. A little too much. In its way it's a historic jewel.'

'It was a little *cadeau d'estime* from the Regent to Great-Great-Grandmama Honoria Ancred,' Cedric cut in. 'Not only historical, but history repeating itself. And *may* I point out, Aunt Pauline, that I personally am rocked to the foundations. I've always understood that the Sunburst was to come to me.'

'To your daughter,' said Paul. 'The point is academic.'

'I'm sure I don't know why you think so,' said Cedric, bridling. 'Anything might happen.'

Paul raised his eyebrows.

'Really, Pauline,' said Millamant. 'Really, Paul!'

'Paul, darling,' said Pauline offensively, 'don't tease poor Cedric.'

'Anyway,' said Fenella, 'I think Aunt Pauline's right. I think he means to marry, and if he does, I'm never coming to Ancreton again. Never!'

'What shall you call her, Aunt Pauline?' Cedric asked impertinently. 'Mummy, or a pet name?'

'There's only one thing to be done,' said Pauline. 'We must tackle him. I've told Jenetta and I've told Dessy. They're both coming. Thomas will have to come too. In Claude's absence he should take the lead. It's his duty.'

'Do you mean, dearest Aunt Pauline, that we are to lie in ambush for the Old Person and make an altogether-boys bounce at him?'

'I propose, Cedric, that we ask him to meet us all and that we simply—we simply—'

'And a fat lot of good, if you'll forgive me for saying so, Pauline, that is likely to do,' said Millamant, with a chuckle.

'Not being an Ancred, Millamant, you can't be expected to feel this terrible thing as painfully as we do. How Papa, with his deep sense of pride in an old name—we go back to the Conquest, Mrs Alleyn—how Papa can have allowed himself to be entangled! It's too humiliating.'

'Not being an Ancred, as you point out, Pauline, I realize Papa, as well as being blue-blooded, is extremely hot-blooded. Moreover, he's as obstinate and vain as a peacock. He likes the idea of himself with a dashing young wife.'

'Comparatively young,' said Cedric.

Pauline clasped her hands, and turning from one member of her family to another, said, 'I've thought of something! Now listen all of you. I'm going to be perfectly frank and impersonal about this. I know I'm the child's mother, but that needn't prevent me. Panty!'

'What about Panty, Mother?' asked Paul nervously.

'Your grandfather adores the child. Now, suppose Panty were just to drop a childish hint.'

'If you suggest,' said Cedric, 'that Panty should wind her little arms round his neck and whisper: "Grandpapa, when will the howwid lady wun away?" I can only say I don't think she'd get into the skin of the part.'

'He adores her,' Pauline repeated angrily. 'He's like a great big boy with her. It brings the tears into my eyes to see them together. You can't deny it, Millamant.'

'I dare say it does, Pauline.'

'Well, but Mother, Panty plays up to Grandpapa,' said Paul bluntly.

'And in any case,' Cedric pointed out, 'isn't Panty as thick as thieves with Sonia?'

'I happen to know,' said Millamant, 'that Miss Orrincourt encouraged Panty to play a very silly trick on me last Sunday.'

'What did she do?' asked Cedric.

Fenella giggled.

'She pinned a very silly notice on the back of my coat when I was going to church,' said Millamant stuffily.

'What did it say, Milly, darling?' Cedric asked greedily.

'Roll out the Barrel,' said Fenella.

'This is getting us nowhere,' said Millamant.

'And now,' said Troy hurriedly, 'I really think if you'll excuse me—'

This time she was able to get away. The Ancreds distract-
edly bade her goodnight. She refused an escort to her room,
and left them barely waiting, she felt, for her to shut the door
before they fell to again.

Only a solitary lamp burned in the hall, which was
completely silent, and since the fire had died out very cold.
While Troy climbed the stairs she felt as she had not felt before
in this enormous house, that it had its own individuality. It
stretched out on all sides of her, an undiscovered territory.
It housed, as well as the eccentricities of the Ancreds, their
deeper thoughts and the thoughts of their predecessors. When
she reached the gallery, which was also dim, she felt that the
drawing-room was now profoundly distant, a subterranean
island. The rows of mediocre portraits and murky landscapes
that she now passed had a life of their own in this half-light
and seemed to be indifferently aware of her progress. Here, at
last, was her own passage with the tower steps at the end. She
halted for a moment before climbing them. Was it imagination,
or had the door, out of sight on the half-landing above her,
been softly closed? 'Perhaps,' she thought, 'somebody lives in
the room below me,' and for some reason the notion affected
her unpleasantly. 'Ridiculous!' thought Troy, and turned on a
switch at the foot of the stairs. A lamp, out of sight beyond the
first spiral, brought the curved wall rather stealthily to life.

Troy mounted briskly, hoping there would still be a fire
in her white room. As she turned the spiral, she gathered up
her long dress with her right hand and with her left reached
out for the narrow rail.

The rail was sticky.

She snatched her hand away with some violence and
looked at it. The palm and the under-surface were dark. Troy
stood in the shadow of the inner wall, but she now moved up
into light. By the single lamps she saw that the stain on her
hand was red.

Five seconds must have gone by before she realized that
the stuff on her hand was paint.

CHAPTER FIVE

The Bloody Child

AT HALF PAST TEN the following morning Troy, hung with paint boxes and carrying a roll of canvas and stretchers, made her way to the little theatre. Guided by Paul and Cedric, who carried her studio easel between them, she went down a long passage that led out of the hall, turned right at a green baize door, 'beyond which,' Cedric panted, 'the Difficult Children ravage at will,' and continued towards the rear of that tortuous house. Their journey was not without incident, for as they passed the door of what, as Troy later discovered, was a small sitting-room, it was flung open and a short plumpish man appeared, his back towards them, shouting angrily: 'If you've no faith in my treatment, Sir Henry, you have an obvious remedy. I shall be glad to be relieved of the thankless task of prescribing for a damned obstinate patient and his grand-daughter.' Troy made a valiant effort to forge ahead, but was blocked by Cedric, who stopped short, holding the easel diagonally across the passage and listening with an air of the liveliest